SURVIVOR DIARIES

DUST STORM!

SURVIVOR DIARIES

DUST STORM!

BY TERRY LYNN JOHNSON

HOUGHTON MIFFLIN HARCOURT
Boston   New York

hmhco.com

The text was set in Adobe Caslon Pro.
Illustrations by Jani Orban

Library of Congress Cataloging-in-Publication Data
Names: Johnson, Terry Lynn, author.
Title: Dust storm! / by Terry Lynn Johnson.
Description: Boston ; New York : Houghton Mifflin Harcourt, [2019] | Series:
Survivor diaries | Summary: Separated from their group during a
sixth-graders geocaching trip, Jen Chiu and her mortal enemy, Martin Diaz,
are caught in a dust storm in the desert near Las Cruces, New Mexico.
Includes survival tips.
Identifiers: LCCN 2017027713 | ISBN 9780544970984 (paper over board)
ISBN 9781328529299 (paperback)
Subjects: | CYAC: Survival—Fiction. | Deserts—Fiction. | Dust
storms—Fiction. | Chihuahuan Desert—Fiction.
Classification: LCC PZ7.J63835 Dus 2019 | DDC [Fic]—dc23
LC record available at https://lccn.loc.gov/2017027713

Printed in the United States of America
DOC 10 9 8 7 6 5 4 3 2 1
4500729101

For my best friend, Denis.
Without you, none of this would be possible.

CHAPTER ONE

"Were you afraid?" The reporter set his phone on the coffee table in front of me and pressed the Record button.

"Of course she was," Ma Ma said, rocking faster in her chair.

I rubbed at a spot on my jeans. My grandparents did not like this story, and I didn't want Ma Ma hearing the details again.

"Aiya," she muttered.

My grandfather placed his hand on her knee, and her frantic rocking slowed. "Let Jen tell it," he said calmly.

"She's a strong, smart girl," Ma Ma said to the reporter. "That's all you need to know."

"Yes, Mrs. Chiu," agreed the reporter. "But I'd like to hear the account in Jen's words. I'm writing a series about resourceful kids like her who have survived a life-threatening experience."

He turned his gaze to me just as I was reaching for one of the mini cream puffs sitting in Mom's fancy dish, the one that she uses only when guests are here. We don't usually have sweets like this. I popped a pastry in my mouth.

The reporter leaned across the coffee table toward me. "Go on and tell me about what happened in the Chihuahuan Desert," he said.

"It was so craz—" A piece of cream puff flew out of my mouth and landed on his phone.

"Aiya," Ma Ma said.

I clamped a hand over my mouth as I swallowed. "I mean . . . it was intense. The air was so full of sand—it felt like a million bees stinging. The wind screamed around us. Grit got into my eyes, up my nose. We couldn't see anything. I'll never forget the roar just before—"

"Jen," the reporter interrupted. "I'd really like to hear the whole story. Start from the beginning. It will help readers know what to do if something like this happens to them. So tell me." His eyebrows rose. "How did you survive?"

I thought about that day. Brought my mind back to the endless desert in New Mexico. Back to the heat and the fear and the terrible thirst.

"It all started with the Snake Byte," I began.

CHAPTER TWO

Two months earlier.

The van jolted over another bump on the dirt road, and I adjusted my earbuds. The trick to being one of only two girls in a van full of sixth-grade geocachers is to look busy. Pretend you're too into your music to care that no one is talking to you.

And definitely pretend you don't miss your new best friend back in Tucson, who couldn't come to this geocaching event because she was going on summer vacation with her family.

At least, that's what she said, but I suspected it had something to do with the name of the event, Snake Byte. Though I told her actual snakes were probably not involved. Judging by the clever name, most likely all our clues for the cache locations were going to have something to do with a *byte*—information in bits of eight.

I peered over the seat in front of me, where my mortal enemy—Martin Diaz—was also sitting alone. He'd been reading a book about New Mexico since we left Tucson. He took forever to flip pages, so I switched between reading the book over his shoulder and looking out the window at the gray landscape. Dead grass, flat-topped mesas, stony ridge faces, and scrubby creosote bushes as far as I could see. The tall, spiky poles of agave plants stood out here and there like punctuation marks.

I hoped that once we got to Las Cruces there would be more exciting terrain, but the only things out there that really mattered to me were the mystery caches. I was going to beat everyone in Club. *Especially* Martin Diaz. Tomorrow, I planned to find all the caches before he did and leave my signature tokens—friendship rings—so he'd realize I'd beat him there. I'd get my name up on the Geocache Superstars chart back at Club. And Martin would have to admit I was awesome. I'd make him wish he was still my best friend.

Not that I cared that he stopped talking to me last year. That was so long ago, I'd almost forgotten about how we used to meet behind our houses and work on our fort in the orange tree. Or how we dressed up in my grandparents' old clothes and put on plays for them. Nope. Didn't care.

Martin flipped the next page, so I could continue reading.

of the Clovis culture of ancient New Mexico.

Today, the Chihuahuan Desert is mainly a *rain shadow desert*. Large mountain ranges on the east and west block the moisture coming from the

oceans. If you are caught in desert climate, it is vi-
tal to keep hydrated. Remember: a gallon of water
per day per person.

🌵 **Avoid sweating**. You lose more moisture when
you sweat.

🌵 **Do not panic**. If you are lost, panic kills. Remain
calm and stay where you are so searchers can
find you. Using a signal mirror is best.

🌵 **Watch the weather**. When storms approach, go
to high ground. Stay out of dry washes and arroyos, which can flood suddenly and

"Hey," Martin said. He slammed the book
closed and glared over his shoulder at me. "Mind
your own business."

I was about to snap back at him when the
van lurched and stopped with an ominous thud.
I pulled out my earbuds and stuffed them in
my pocket. I could hear the wheels spinning,
but we weren't moving. Everyone started yelling, and Mr. Lee jumped up to speak with the
driver.

"Calm down, people," Mr. Lee said. "Stay

here while we sort this out." He hopped out with the driver to look at the rutted road.

Everyone crammed to one side of the van to peer out the windows.

"Yup. We're stuck. Should've let me drive."

"As if you can drive, Alonzo."

I tried to stay out of the way of the guys clowning and shoving one another.

"We're all gonna die!"

"Don't be stupid. It's probably a flat tire. Look."

Outside, Mr. Lee pointed his cell phone in the air. He wandered around until he gave up and popped his head back in the van.

"Hey, everybody. We're stuck. But the cache starting point isn't far. I'm going ahead to see what other teams have arrived and to get assistance. You will *stay* here with Mrs. Sloan and help her set up the shade tarp. I expect my cachers to be on their best behavior." He eyeballed us. "I'll be back shortly." As he prepared to go, he muttered something about talking to whoever organized the event and picked a location with such bad roads.

We all filed out to help Mrs. Sloan with the tarp. The heat of the day draped over me as soon as I stepped out of the air-conditioned van. I could see how the tires of the van and the trailer had wedged into a deep rut on the shoulder of the road. We were going to need a tow truck.

I pulled out my cell phone to text Mom. I wanted her to tell me this kind of thing happened all the time and not to worry.

But no bars. No network. I clutched the phone and then stuffed it in my backpack.

Once we all got used to the idea that we were stuck here, we gathered around Mrs. Sloan, who brought out a cooler from the trailer. I realized I didn't need my pack, so I went back to stash it in the van. Just before I opened the door, I spied the top of Martin's head through the window. Why was he hiding in the van?

CHAPTER THREE

Martin was bent over Mr. Lee's briefcase. I let out a silent hiss. Were the cache coordinates in there? If Martin knew the latitudes and longitudes, he could skip having to solve the clues before getting the directions to the caches. He'd get to all the caches before me. I watched as Martin pulled out his Global Positioning System unit. Was he cheating and entering the lats and longs into his GPS?

I ducked down when Martin's head swiveled around. He stuffed his GPS in his pocket as if he realized he could get caught. I barely had time to slip around the hood of the van and hide before Martin jumped out and darted to the trailer.

While he was gone, I crept into the front seat to take a look at what he'd been doing. But Mr. Lee's briefcase was closed and there wasn't any evidence of Martin being in there. I tossed my pack on my seat and snuck back out. When I glanced at Mrs. Sloan, she had her head in the cooler as she passed around water bottles.

While I watched, Martin jumped out of the trailer with his mountain bike. He ran toward the ditch on the opposite side of the van from where everyone else was sitting in the shade. When he glanced over his shoulder, I edged behind the van. Martin bolted up the incline, crested the hill, and disappeared from view.

He must have thought he could find one of the caches and exchange his dumb snake-tattoo tokens before anyone else had a chance. He'd get his pick at the best tokens in the cache box. But worse, if he had all the cache locations, he'd beat me. I was not going to let that happen. I had to stop him!

My stomach jumped with nerves as I raced to the trailer and freed my bike. I grabbed my helmet and got ready to make a run for it. I had to time it right. As soon as Mrs. Sloan's head was in the cooler again, I dashed up the hill and over the bank.

Once I was out of sight of the rest of the group, I had a chance to look around. I was in a basin with desert sprawling out in all directions. There were no trees here like at home. No tall saguaro cactus, only shrubby bushes dotting the gravelly dirt baked hard and crunchy underfoot. The desert sun felt white-hot. I shaded my eyes against the glare, searching. There was Martin, pedaling away from me, his silver helmet bobbing up and down. I hopped on my bike and raced after him.

I had to concentrate on steering around low thorny bushes. Martin seemed busy doing the same thing; he didn't look behind him once.

He was definitely going to a cache. Why else would he have snuck off with his bike into the middle of the desert? He must have entered the coordinates into his GPS. What a jerk! If I could get his GPS out of the mount on his handlebars, I could prove it. He'd be busted.

I sped up to catch him. Sweat trickled out from my helmet and ran down my temples but dried instantly on my face. The thirsty air sucked up any moisture. Martin was so focused on the terrain and his GPS, he didn't hear me until I came up beside him.

"Whatcha doin'?" I asked sweetly. He jumped as if he'd been electrocuted, then turned red. I pointed at him. "You're not cheating, are you? That would be poor form, even for you."

Martin huffed and stammered. It seemed to take a while for his brain to assess the situation. He shoved his hand in his pocket and said, "I can show them to you, too. We'd be the only ones who know." I glanced at the sheet he pulled out.

JUNE, Las Cruces, New Mexico

Mystery Cache Event: SNAKE BYTE – Coordinates list

Martin turned his GPS toward me. "See? This first cache isn't far from here! It says it's only point-five miles that way."

My gaze followed where he pointed. "We shouldn't be—" I stopped when I noticed the sky. It looked as if something big had exploded far behind us.

And then I saw it—a wall of dirt rose high in the air. So high, it blocked out the sun.

"What *is* that?" Martin shaded his eyes and stared at the debris in the air.

"Does it look like it's moving toward us?" I said, a flutter of panic in my chest.

A sudden gust of wind hit us hard and almost knocked us off our bikes. Our eyes met, full of horror.

I whipped around and gripped my handlebars. "Ride!" I yelled, but my words were swept away in the wail of the wind.

CHAPTER FOUR

When I glanced back at the cloud, I saw it had grown like a swarm of pale yellow locusts. And it was gaining on us.

I knew what it was then. And it was bigger than anything I'd seen before.

"Dust storm!" Martin screamed.

We dashed away on our bikes, trying to get ahead of it. Maybe we could outride it. Racing over uneven ground, I struggled to keep hold of my handlebars. *Don't crash into that prickly pear cactus! Keep focused. Watch out for those rocks!*

Don't look back.

"Come on!" I yelled to Martin.

I pedaled like a cyclone, pumping my legs as hard as I could. Had to be far ahead of it by now. I'd never ridden so fast. Couldn't look behind me. No time to slow down. But how close was it?

I glanced back just as a giant wall of choking dust hit us.

I squinted my eyes half closed, but sand and grit flew in, blinding me. My eyes burned. The storm flayed my skin. My loose hair lashed the sides of my face.

The air was thick with sand. I could hardly breathe. Choking on grit, I covered my nose with one hand, but then I couldn't keep my bike straight.

Wind whipped my T-shirt. Furious gusts filled it with sand.

All I could see was sand. I'd lost sight of Martin. I was in my own world full of stinging and choking. Everything around me was gone. I hoped I was riding in a straight line.

Something sharp and prickly scraped my ankle as I rode by. I opened my mouth to scream, but it filled with sand.

Choking!

I gagged and spit. Pressed my gritty lips together tightly.

My skin was on fire. Sand in the air, stinging like hornets. I had no idea where Martin had gone.

I saw a dark object, coming closer. Wait. Was that him?

A broken tree trunk flew through the air, narrowly missing me. It bounced on the ground, branches exploding in all directions, then disappeared as quickly as it had come.

I stopped, feet off the pedals, hands over my burning eyes. *Make it stop!* I was being eaten alive by the desert. My heart hammered. I could feel my whole body quaking.

The roar of the wind was like a jet plane. I'd seen dust storms before back home but usually watched them through a window. A storm was completely different out here in the middle of it. Out here I could hear it growl, feel its teeth, and taste its grit.

I knew I should get off my bike and crouch down. If I stopped, I'd have both hands free. I wanted to shield my ears, and my eyes and nose. I could hide in my shirt.

But I didn't want Martin to leave me out here. I didn't want to be stuck in the desert without my bike. I didn't want to be in this storm alone. The last time I'd seen Martin, he was riding away from the dust storm. I didn't know where to go, but I had to get away too. I cracked open my eyes into slits and started forward again.

Where was Martin? I couldn't hear him. I couldn't yell for him. Couldn't open my mouth. He wouldn't even hear me over the shrieking wind.

Suddenly, there he was. Martin, next to me, a ghost in a cloud. We almost crashed, riding beside each other, and then we broke apart again. He vanished into the sand.

I heard a wail. Was that Martin yelling something, or the wind? Where was that noise coming from? The wind roared in my head.

But that sound again. More wailing. Something was very wrong with that noise.

I pedaled straight into the driving, biting sand. And then my bike fell out from under me. I was in the air and falling blind.

I had ridden off a cliff.

CHAPTER FIVE

I was falling through the air.

As I dropped, my stomach lurched into my throat.

And then I crashed.

My bike crumpled underneath me. Broke my fall. My face slammed into something hard; my eyes watered from the pain. I let out a grunt and rolled off the bike. I unclipped my helmet with a shaky hand. It felt as if I'd just stepped off a roller coaster and my body was trying to catch up to the stillness. I lay there a moment, dazed and pounding, a pile of dried bones.

Carefully, I lifted my head and looked around. The dust storm howled above, but down here it was less fierce. I could see the outline of something several feet away. I struggled to my hands and knees and crawled toward it. Every part of me stung something awful. My ankle burned where I'd been scraped by the sharp thing. I kept crawling.

"Martin!"

He was crumpled in a heap next to his bike. I reached for his shoulder and squeezed it. He moaned. When his head came up, I let out a breath in relief.

We crouched together while the wind and sand flew by. I spat out the grit in my mouth. Closed my eyes, scratched and raw. My nerves tingled, and my heart beat a loud rhythmic base in my ears. I tried singing in my head to pretend I wasn't here; to pretend the screaming dread I felt wasn't real. I rubbed at my nose, still throbbing from my fall. My helmet probably saved it from being bashed in.

Finally, the storm began to weaken. The wind stopped shrieking as abruptly as it had started. Martin and I broke apart and looked around, blinking. My ears rang in the sudden silence. We were in a deep, narrow gorge. Dry sand and dust settled over everything in a thick coating.

Martin and I struggled to our feet. My head hurt. My skin stung. I was bleeding from my ankle and nose and from cuts on my hands. My eyes felt swollen. Martin had a fat lip and red, swollen eyes. He ripped off his helmet and threw it on the ground. The wide-brimmed hat he wore underneath was curled up at the front.

I reached down in a bit of a daze to pluck out three cactus spines stuck through my sock into my skin. "Yow!"

My yell startled Martin into action. "My bike!" he cried, kneeling beside his broken bike. "I'm so dead," he said. "Dad just got me this."

The front wheel was mangled and bent backward. I felt a moment of sympathy for him, since I'd seen his dad get angry. Then I stumbled to my own bike to assess the damage. Front fork angled down, front wheel sharply bent, handlebars shoved back.

"Is your GPS okay?" I asked.

"It's gone!" Martin began searching in the dirt. "Oh, no. I'm really dead now."

I peered around. "Where are we?" I looked up at the steep walls on either side of us. As tall as the clay-tiled roof of my house back home. We were in a snaking ravine that looked like something out of *Star Wars*.

"We're in an arroyo," Martin said.

Of course. This was what happened in a desert when rain fell hard and gouged out a path. That's why there were roots sticking out of the walls as if a giant bulldozer had been through here. But the rain that created this had long since dried up. Everything was dirt-dry and barren, covered in dust. The high walls were steep on both sides.

"Come on," Martin said, trying to claw his way up the bank. "We have to get up top. I can't tell where we are down here." He grasped roots, slipped, and fell back.

We both tried to climb but quickly discovered the bank was too steep and too high, with loose rocks and unstable sand. Looking up at the dark clouds in the sky, I recalled what I'd read in Martin's book in the van.

"Hey! We were just in a dust storm."

"Well, duh. You think?"

I glared at him. "We can't be down here! Don't dust storms travel in front of thunderstorms? That storm might've dumped rain somewhere else! Even if it was ten miles away, the runoff will race down a gut like this arroyo. This is the worst place to be after a storm! We need to get to high ground."

Martin glanced around, alarmed. I could see he knew I was right.

"We have to go. Now, now, now. Have to get out of here," Martin said in a panicked voice.

"Wait." I reached for my bike to see if there was anything I could save. My helmet lay next

to it and looked like it was cracked. Useless. I didn't want to leave my bike here, but with the tire like this, I couldn't even push it. And we had no time. Less than no time. We had to get out of here right now.

We had only two choices. Since we couldn't climb out, we had to follow one of the directions the arroyo led. I looked to my left and then to my right. In this twisty corridor, I could see only as far as the next bend. Martin started running to our left.

I hesitated. "How do you know which way to go?"

"This feels right!" Martin was almost around the corner. With a last look back, I raced after him.

We sprinted along the arroyo, skirting rocks and heaps of dirt. I felt like any minute we'd hear the roar of a giant wave coming at us like a demon at our heels.

Trickling water is how it would start, and then more and more until a rush of rainwater would sweep us away. We'd have nowhere to go. We'd drown in a raging river, trapped in this arroyo.

Calm down, I told myself. *That's not going to happen.*

My feet pounded on the dirt. My back tingled with the anticipation of rushing water slamming into it. I strained to listen for the sound of a flood surging behind us.

The arroyo went on and on, twisting this way and that. We raced to each bend, hoping we'd see a way out, but the high walls continued looming over us. It felt like we'd been trapped down here for hours. I glanced at the sky again. The sight of the storm clouds ignited fresh panic in me, and I bolted forward. My lips were still gritty as I panted in the heat.

"Here!" Martin yelled up ahead. He'd finally found a place in the wall where it had collapsed, creating a foothold we could climb.

We scrambled up the loose dirt. Sharp things poked my fingers as I grabbed hold. Finally, I pulled myself up over the rim and out of danger. I peered down at where we'd just been trapped, sighing a big relieved breath. Martin and I brushed ourselves off and glanced at each other, then turned to see where we were.

Distant, unfamiliar mountains surrounded us. Dirt with gravelly patches between the creosote bushes stretched out to the horizon. Everything was flat and empty, save for a hawk flying low to the ground.

"Where are we?" Martin asked quietly.

Dread crashed through me. Even though we could see around us now, we had no way to tell which direction to go.

CHAPTER SIX

"Where *are* we?" Martin asked again, louder.

When our eyes met, I could see my own fear reflecting back.

"Help!" I yelled. Maybe Mrs. Sloan and Mr. Lee were out looking for us in the van. I wished I'd grabbed a bottle of water from the cooler. "We're here!"

All I could hear were a few birds in the nearby bushes. I tried to swallow; my throat felt like sandpaper. Grit from the dust storm was still in my mouth, coating my tongue.

"I think the van is that way," Martin said, pointing straight ahead.

"No, it feels like this way," I said, pointing to the left.

No matter which way we looked, there were no landmarks other than the mountains all around us. Where was the van? Which way should we go? Everything looked and felt the same. Shrub brush and gravel, grass the color of straw, and flat ridges. No sense of direction. Just heat so heavy, it felt like it was grinding me into the earth.

I could feel the panic clawing through my mind. At least the sun was hidden behind the clouds that hung darkly in the distance.

As I thought this, the sun broke free and beat down on my bare head. I shielded my eyes, wishing I'd brought my helmet with me even if it was cracked, just to cover my head. Ye Ye, my grandfather, had helped me pick it out at the mall. Now I really regretted leaving it in the arroyo.

Still, the worst thing? We had no water.

"What are we going to do?" Martin yelled. He was breathing fast.

"We have to stay calm, no matter what," I said, searching around. "The book said 'panic kills.'"

"What?" Martin's fists clenched.

I turned to him, and something shiny beyond him caught my eye: a glint of sun reflecting off the blades of a windmill.

"Look!" I said, pointing. "Windmills pump water. That's the most important thing right now. We need a gallon of water per person per day in the desert."

"How do you know? Where did you hear that?"

"From your book! Don't you remember? You read it too." My memory had always been sharp. My brain took pictures like a phone, and I could scroll through mental photos of things I'd read or seen. It was helpful, but also frustrating when others couldn't remember the same.

My words made Martin angrier. "Well, why didn't you bring any water, then, if you're so smart?"

"We wouldn't even be here if you hadn't snooped in Mr. Lee's things!" I reminded him. "Let's just head to the windmill. Once we find some water, we can make a plan for what we're going to do."

As we walked, I tried licking my lips. My mouth felt pasty.

"The main thing about being in the desert is conserving water," I said. "We have to protect the water that's already inside us. No more running. We need to stop sweating."

"How're we going to do that?" Martin demanded. "It's a bazillion degrees out here. And you're the one who said we had to get out of the arroyo fast."

"I know. At least you still have your hat," I said, eyeing his wide-brimmed hat. Just seeing it made my cheeks and nose burn hotter.

The sun baked my brains. My head pounded

and my face felt stiff, caked in dried sweat over the dust.

Martin glanced at me. "Where's your hat? You need one."

"If I could make one out of a cactus, I'd be all set." I sat down on a boulder to empty gravel out of my shoe. I inspected my ankle that had the cactus spines in it. All at once, all my scrapes and cuts seemed to throb. My nose stung from the fall into the arroyo. I rubbed at a cut on my palm as a whimper escaped me.

Martin bent toward me. I showed him the gash.

Martin made a tsking noise and straightened up. "It doesn't look that bad! Quit whining, and come on."

I stood, wiping my nose. "I'm not whining! I've got cuts all over me, and they could get infected!" I was close to tears, which made me angry. I didn't want to cry in front of Martin. I didn't want him to think I was a baby. "Why do you hate me?"

Martin shook his head. "I'm thirsty and sweating. We need to stop talking." He stalked ahead.

For a while, neither of us spoke. The only sound was our crunching footsteps and some clicking from an insect in the brush around us.

I wanted my mom. I wanted her to fuss over my hand. She'd draw a happy face on a Band-Aid and stick it over the cut.

Martin slowed, then stopped walking. He glanced at me again and then took off his blue striped shirt.

"What are you doing?" I said. "We need to keep the sun off us as much as possible." We both had on short-sleeved shirts, which I knew weren't as good as long sleeves out here. But at least we both had on long pants.

Martin ignored me and peeled off his T-shirt next.

"Here." He shoved the T-shirt at me. It was the same tan color as the ground surrounding us. "You can cover your head at least." He put his striped shirt back on and buttoned it up to his neck.

"Thank you," I managed to say. I wrapped the shirt over my head, even though it smelled like boy. It helped. I bent to tuck my pants into my socks. My running shoes wouldn't keep snakes from biting me, but I could try to keep out the sand. Grit rubbed between my toes and in my heels. It got in everywhere.

My eyes still burned from the dust storm. The bright sun glaring off the earth around us made them feel even worse. I wished I had sunglasses. The shirt I wore on my head partially shaded my eyes, but not as well as the brim on Martin's hat. Still, I could see him squinting painfully. The sun was too intense. Glancing at the sky, I searched for the clouds and hoped they'd drift closer. Maybe they would bring rain. Or they could break up or move farther away.

We walked for what felt like miles. I tried to ignore how thirsty I was. Martin was right. To stop our saliva from evaporating, we needed to keep our mouths closed. Mine felt so parched, my tongue hurt. Why didn't I bring water? Why did we leave the group at all?

All I knew was that the windmill was our only hope.

The windmill didn't look that far when I first saw it. My raging thirst was all I could think about. That and how hot I was. In the city, I could always go into an air-conditioned store, or ride in a car with the air blasting me in the face. Out here, there was nowhere to go. Nowhere to hide in this big wide open. Miles of hot.

By the time we stumbled over the last ridge and peered down at the windmill, I felt dizzy and weak. I could hardly collect spit in my mouth to swallow.

At last we would have water. Then we'd be able to think. Be able to come up with a plan for what we were going to do.

We staggered toward the windmill and

reached for the oval tank where the water collected. When we bent over the galvanized steel
sides, we both gasped.

The tank was dry.

CHAPTER SEVEN

"We're dead," Martin said. "There's no water here. We're going to die of thirst."

"Let's calm down and think about this."

"This is your fault." He turned and jabbed a finger at me. "'Follow the windmill,' you said. 'There'll be water there,' you said. With you around, it's a wonder we're even alive."

His words hung in the air. They made everything seem worse. He was right. We actually could die out here. My heart fluttered just thinking about the trouble we were in.

"Well, it was in your book," I said. "Why are you acting like I'm the only one who read it?"

Martin pretended he didn't hear me. He studied the lever on the side of the metal frame before yanking at it. "This is supposed to unlock the blades." He peered up at the windmill blades and pointed with renewed interest. "I see another lever up by the gear box. This one must be broken. I'll climb up and start it."

Martin grabbed a rung on the frame and pulled himself up. When he reached the top, he did something that made the wind vane spring out. The blades caught the hot breeze and began to turn. A rhythmic clanking came from the pole as it moved up and down in the center.

"Yay!" I cheered.

"Is there water?" he called down.

I watched the tank with a hope so sharp it hurt. "No," I said. "It's pumping dust."

Martin descended in a huff, not watching his footing. He missed a step and fell into the palo verde bush growing next to the frame.

"Stupid ladder!" He struggled up out of the bush. When he stood, I gaped at him. He was covered in prickly-looking balls. They stuck to his shirt, his pants, the skin on his arms. He looked like a hedgehog.

"Cholla cactus! It got me!" He hopped around in a panic. "Get them out!"

"Stand still; let me see."

He brushed at the balls frantically, which made them stick to his hands. "Augh! Help! Get them off." He rubbed his hands against the windmill frame, and the balls dislodged and dropped.

I struggled not to laugh at his flailing. "How can I help when you're dancing around?"

He held out his prickly hands. "Don't touch them. They'll stick into you, too."

I spied two flat rocks on the ground. "We can use these. Show me your arm."

Martin stood still long enough for me to check the cactus balls on his arm. The spines were embedded in his skin. He had three balls stuck in his bare skin, and four more through his shirt and pants.

"Careful, careful," Martin said.

I lined the rocks on either side of one cactus ball on his arm like a giant tweezer. In a quick motion, I flicked it off.

"OW!"

The ball just rolled down Martin's arm and embedded again. I flicked it harder.

"AUGH!"

It flew to the ground, leaving behind welling dots of blood. "Got it!" I said, and before he could move again, I flicked the next one.

"Yowch! Wait! Give me some warning!" Martin clutched his arm and inspected the wounds. A few cactus spines were still in his hands. He grasped one and yanked.

"*Ah!*" he yelled with each spine that he ripped out. Then he took a deep breath. "It feels like my skin is on fire. But keep going."

I continued flicking off the cactus. Martin screamed and bled. I was *so* not going anywhere near a cactus after this.

I inspected Martin's back. "Only a few more balls left." As soon as I said it, I was reminded of a couple Christmases ago when Martin and I had to wrestle my cat.

Momo had jumped into a box filled with tiny Styrofoam balls. The expression of shock on Momo's face was enough to send us into hysterics, even though he didn't like to be laughed at.

With the pink Styrofoam balls clinging to his long black hair, he completely lost his cool. He dashed around wildly trying to shake them off. The whole time, his convulsing matched the beat of an oldies song Dad had on the stereo, "Great Balls of Fire."

"Goodness, gracious, great balls of fire," I sang now under my breath.

Martin muffled a laugh, which made me start to giggle.

"At least they're not pink," Martin said.

Then we were laughing like old times. But when I flicked the last cactus ball out of Martin's back, his laughter turned to tears.

The last time I'd seen Martin cry was when we dared each other to bike down Suicide Hill with no hands. I'd walked our bikes back after he crashed and ran home crying.

It scared me that he cried now. I needed something to look at besides him. Peering closer at one of the rocks in my hand, I noticed it was shaped like a spearhead. I turned it over in my hands, and the edge nicked me like a knife. "Hey, this is a Clovis point."

"A what?"

"You know, the Clovis people in history? The first settlers? This is an ancient tool over thirteen thousand years old, and it's still sharp! How cool is that?"

"What are you talking about?"

"Your book! It was in the book you were reading about New Mexico."

Martin sniffed, gave me a funny look, and then ignored me. He pulled a sheet out of his pocket. It was the coordinate sheet for the Snake Byte cache locations.

"How is that going to help?" I asked.

"I'm trying to figure out where we are. The coordinates show the caches aren't far from each other." Martin squatted and started drawing lines in the dirt. "That first Snake Byte cache was a half mile from the road, here." He poked a dot not far from the line he made. "And this was the arroyo we fell into."

I knelt beside him, and we both studied the drawing. "The road was more like this," I said, drawing the curve I remembered from the map. "It came off the highway here."

"If we look at these other cache locations, you can see they're all around the same area." He pointed to the page. "Like, this one is just west of the first one I punched into the GPS." Martin examined the lines in the dirt. "The co-ordinate is zero-point-zero-one degrees away from the first. That means it's a little over half a mile away, around here." He indicated a place on the ground over a clump of short cactus. "So there's probably a road close to where they set up all those caches."

"How can you tell that without your GPS?"

Martin looked up in surprise. "Because of the coordinates. Look: they're just a few numbers different."

I stared at the coordinates listed on the sheet. "I've never thought about what the numbers mean. I just put them into the GPS, and it tells me which way to go." I grinned sheepishly, but he only scowled back as if I'd offended him.

Martin glared at the lines in the dirt again. "Did you draw this road exactly in the direction it was on the map?"

"Yes," I said. Now it was my turn to be annoyed. Martin knew how my memory worked.

"So . . . if we're somewhere around here, we need to walk in a straight line, due southeast, and we'll cross this highway." He stood and looked around, shading his eyes. "I wish I had a compass."

"A GPS would be handy," I said.

Martin pointed. "Sun's setting over there, so that means that direction is west. More or less." Then he turned toward our left. "And this is south. Let's get going." He toed something out of the dirt at his feet, then picked up a short steel pole. "Can use this for snake protection." He swung it experimentally.

I remembered that Martin's book said if you got lost, you should stay still so rescuers could find you. But we had no water. The pounding in my head told me we needed water, and soon. I glanced anxiously around and saw that daylight was fading. Martin was right again. We had to find our way out of the desert before it got dark.

Despite how thirsty we were, we had to keep walking. We'd surely die from dehydration if we stayed here.

CHAPTER EIGHT

"It'll be cooler walking without the sun, at least," I said. Despite the promising clouds earlier, they had eventually drifted off.

The desert seemed to be waking up around us. A large bird that could have been a roadrunner flew between the shrubs on my left. A rabbit burst out near our feet and dashed away.

The sky was a soft ocean blue turning rose pink over the mountain. Beyond the shrubs was a ridge that had simply looked like dirt earlier, but now with the muted light glowing on it, I could see the bands of rust red, orange, and yellow. The sound of crickets was everywhere.

As we crunched over dead grass and hard dirt, I wondered if the club had made it to the meeting point and found the other teams. If a tow truck had gotten the van unstuck. Everyone might be at the hotel in Las Cruces by now. They'd have had supper, had something to drink. I tried licking my lips again.

The games they'd planned for tonight were probably canceled because we were missing. In fact, maybe the whole event would be canceled. They must've called my dad at the courthouse. I wondered if he was in the middle of a trial. Mom might've been out walking with my baby brother, Jack, and Ma Ma, my grandmother.

I wondered who was out looking for us right now. I was sure they had canteens of water. Gallons of it. Maybe they were right over the hill, just about to find us. They were probably going to find us very soon.

What I wouldn't have given for water right now. I'd never been so thirsty in my life. I didn't even notice missing supper. I just wanted to drink.

I rubbed my burning eyes. They felt like they still had grit in them, and I was having trouble seeing. I strained to find Martin in the low light.

"Slow down!" I called to him, stepping over piles of dried-up dung. It was everywhere. "I don't want to bump into a cactus in the dark." Soon we weren't going to be able to see anything. Where was the road? Where were the people or towns? The desert was a huge space filled with nothing.

The darker it became, the closer Martin and I shifted toward each other. I glanced down at another dried-up cow patty, but as I watched, it uncoiled itself and slithered away.

"Snake!" I stopped dead, electric fear charging through me. "We can't keep walking when we can't see anything." My heart pounded. "There could be rattlers anywhere!"

"Yeah, okay." Martin bent over and used his prod to scrape a clear spot on the sand where we could rest. When he straightened again, he grabbed his head. "Ugh. I stood too fast. I'm dizzy."

Growing up in Tucson, everyone knew the signs of dehydration. It made you lightheaded. But there wasn't anything we could do about it out here.

I sat down, feeling sick to my stomach. Sitting was worse. The sand was hot. And now that I was still, I noticed the noises all around us. Things were coming out in the darkness. I wondered about scorpions and snakes and biting lizards.

When we heard the howls and yipping behind us, we locked eyes.

"We need a fire," Martin said. "I wish I had matches."

"Hey!" I pulled the Clovis point out of my pocket. "This is flint. Your snake prod is made of steel. We can make a fire with flint and steel!"

"Really?" Martin picked up his steel prod. "How?"

The coyotes seemed to answer. Their many voices sang an ominous song not far over the ridge.

"We need fuel," I said. "Collect some wood. Maybe some of these dried cowpies, but watch that they're not snakes! Try those tall stalks. Oh, but we need tinder first." I talked as though I'd done this before. Doing something was easier when you were confident. "To make a fire, we need ignition, tinder, and fuel. Do you have any lint in your pockets?" I found a little ball of it in my left front pocket. Would it be enough to ignite a spark?

Martin pulled the Snake Byte papers with the cache coordinates from his pocket.

"Oh, yeah. That'll work," I said.

He ripped the bottom of the page and crumpled it up before tossing it on our pile. Once we had the fuel and tinder ready, I crouched over with the steel and flint.

"You just have to hit them together, and it creates sparks," I said, trying to sound sure. "Ye Ye told me about how he had to make fire with flint and steel back when he was younger. I looked it up because I wasn't sure if he was telling stories. You know how he is."

Even though it was a while ago, I clearly remembered reading about flint and steel as if I had a website in my brain. But I had only read about it. I had never actually tried it.

CHAPTER NINE

I scraped the rock against the steel rod and was rewarded with a few sparks that were bright in the darkness.

"That's it," Martin said, excited. He glanced behind us.

The coyotes chose that moment to howl and yip again. They sounded like a large pack, and they were closer.

"They're coming," Martin said, waving his arms. "Hurry!"

I frantically sparked the steel and flint together. After a few tries, I figured out I needed to hold the flint down with one hand and strike it with the steel at a certain angle. *Clack. Clack. Clack. Clack.*

A gust of wind blew our tinder around. "We need to protect the fire from the wind," I said.

As Martin gathered stones to build a small rock wall, I leaned over the tinder and made sparks. Over and over again. Reading about making a fire was much easier than actually doing it. The sparks were coming out. Why weren't they lighting?

More coyotes yipped. The sound filled me with panic.

I tried to calm my breathing. I needed to concentrate on making this fire. A shadow ran by. I couldn't look.

"They're right here!" Martin yelled. "Come on, come on!"

CLACK CLACK CLACK CLACK.

My hands shook from the adrenaline coursing through me. I had heard coyotes from inside my house before, but the sound of them outside in the dark was way more terrifying.

Finally, I aimed a long, hot spark into the center of the paper, and it smoldered. I blew on it gently until a tiny burst of flame flared.

"Careful, not too much or you'll smother it," I said as Martin fed it some dried twigs.

Once it caught hold, we could see pairs of green eyes flashing in the firelight.

"Do coyotes eat people?" Martin asked.

"I don't think so," I said. But that wasn't much comfort. The dark made eerie noises seem so much worse, and the only thing between us and the coyotes was the fire.

We crowded as close to the fire as we could, feeding it fuel. We'd need to collect more for the night. We had to keep the darkness away.

"I wonder if they told my parents I'm missing yet," Martin said. "Dad will be mad. Mom's probably crying."

"They must have everyone from Search and Rescue out for us," I said loudly. If I said it loud enough, maybe someone would hear me and find us. Right now would be good. "We'll be home soon."

I thought of my baby brother, Jack. The fine hair covering his warm, soft head always smelled so good. I thought of Ma Ma, Ye Ye, Mom, and Dad, my bedroom with my gummy-bear nightlight. My throat tightened, and I quickly shook my head.

I picked up the outer piece of a wood stalk that grew tall out of some of the plants. It had two hollow bulges shaped like a figure eight that made me pause. Instead of feeding it to the fire, I used the Clovis point to poke it. The sharp stone carved into the wood. "Hey. I can make sunglasses with this!" I held it up in front of my eyes.

"Don't you need glass to make sunglasses?"

"I've seen pictures of people in the arctic wearing goggles with slits in them to keep from snow blindness," I said. "I think we need the same thing to keep from going sand-blind. I just have to cut the end off here and carve two slits to see out!" I held the wood up to the light of the fire.

Just as I started to scrape, I heard a branch crack right behind us. I spun around and peered into the darkness.

"What was that?" I asked. At the same time, a snort came from the bushes.

"What *is* that?" Martin said. He picked up the steel rod and held it in front of him.

Wordlessly we moved closer to each other and sat with our backs touching. Whatever was out there, it sounded bigger than a coyote.

After a tense few minutes when we heard no other sounds, Martin moved away. He slumped over listlessly next to the fire. Both of us were hurting, feeling the effects of having nothing to drink all afternoon. I didn't want to think about what would happen once the sun came out tomorrow. My muscles were already clenching. I needed water like I needed air.

I looked up and caught my breath at the millions of white stars burning and twinkling overhead. "The sky is so big," I said in a whisper.

"The desert is big too," Martin whispered back.

Glancing behind me again, I picked up my sand goggles. I listened for any more weird sounds. There was a loud chorus of crickets. An owl hooted in the distance. A light *tap-tap-tap* came from the other side of Martin.

I kept guard over the fire as I carved slits into the wood with my Clovis point.

CHAPTER TEN

Something was breathing on me.

I opened my eyes. And screamed. Martin, sleeping near me, bolted up, screaming too. A large hulking thing loomed over me, its long face hanging inches above mine.

"HAW-EEEE!" The creature jerked a few steps away, letting me get a better look at it.

"Is that a donkey?" I pointed to the compact little animal. For such a scary beast, it had soft eyes set in a thoughtful gray face.

"I think it's a burro," Martin said, hastily rolling to his feet. He held out a hand toward the animal, but it tossed its head and sidestepped out of reach. "Looks like a wild one."

Next to me, the burnt remains of last night's fire gave off a smoky odor. The night had been colder than I expected, and I'd been glad for the fire. How could the desert be so hot and then turn so cold? I'd never spent the night out in the open like this before. We didn't even have a tent.

I rubbed my ankle where the cactus had got me and surveyed our makeshift camp. The sun was already up but hiding behind clouds. I hoped again for rain. Any drop of water that would help me peel my tongue off the roof of my mouth or soothe my swollen, cracked lips.

"Aiya," I said. I hurt all over. My voice sounded like a croaking frog with a mouth full of pebbles. I eyed the donkey from where I sat. A glance beneath her tail informed me she was female.

"A wild donkey. Huh. I wonder what she wants with us?" I rose and tried to approach her, but the donkey avoided me, too.

"Hawww-eee. HAWWW-EEEEEE."

"Probably wants food," Martin offered.

"HAWWWWW-ee." Her nostrils flared wide toward me.

"Maybe if we catch her, we can ride the donkey out of here," I said.

"Burro." Martin groaned and covered his eyes. "Ow. My eyes feel like they're all scratched."

"That's what I was telling you. We're going sun-blind." I waved the sand goggles I had finished. "But I only made one of these."

"Figures." Martin squinted at me and then pulled his hat down low.

I rubbed my face, which was caked with dried salt. My head felt muzzy and weird when I turned it. But I caught the movement of Donkey as she walked away. "Come on! We have to catch our ride."

"We could catch her easy if we had food to offer," Martin said, joining me.

"I wish we had food," I said.

"I wish we had water."

"I wish we knew where we were," I said.

"I wish we'd stayed at the windmill," Martin said. "It feels like we've been walking in circles ever since. I can't even tell which direction to go now."

I tied my goggles on with the lace out of one of my shoes and looked around. "Hey! I can totally see through the slits. I wasn't sure if I made them too small. My eyes feel better already. We can take turns with the goggles. Even with your hat, you need protection from the glare."

The donkey walked up an incline. As we followed her, our feet spun clumsily in the sand. My shoe that was missing a lace filled with annoying little pebbles.

"Ah!" Martin suddenly clutched his calf and fell over.

"What?" I asked in a panic. "Snake?" I tried to run to him but was overcome with dizziness. A wave of nausea hit me, and I bent over, breathing hard.

Martin rubbed his leg. "My calf muscle just cramped up." He got slowly to his feet and looked about as sick as I felt.

"Your muscles are cramping because we need water," I said, my voice gritty. His lips were peeling, and every part of me ached for something to drink. All my thoughts and actions felt sluggish, like I was in a bad dream, struggling through wet cement. I wasn't sure how much farther either of us could go.

We were so close to the donkey now that we

could almost touch her. She twitched her ears and eyed me over her back.

"Haaw-eeeee." Her nostrils opened wide and round and then relaxed.

"If she would just stop for a moment, I could convince her we're friendly," I said, following after her. "Getting to ride anything would be a relief. Even a ride on a donkey."

"Burro."

I kicked a tin can and bent to pick it up. How did this get out here? I wondered if I could use this to lure the donkey somehow. Maybe pretend it still had food in it. When I straightened up again, I almost dropped the can in excitement.

"Martin, look!" I pointed. The donkey was heading toward a row of willows. They grew together in a line, along with other small bushes. It was the most green we'd seen since we'd been out here.

"What?" He shaded his eyes. Our clouds

had broken up, and the broiling sun blazed down.

"Come on!" I stumbled faster toward the trees.

"What is it? I thought we weren't supposed to run." Martin lurched after me.

When we crested the rise, we could see down to where a shallow arroyo snaked across the terrain. It looked like a river, but without the water.

"Willows mean water," I said. Donkey stood at the outer bend of the wash and pawed the ground.

"What's she doing?" When Martin and I rushed forward, her head came up to look at us. Her white muzzle dripped with water.

We threw ourselves down the cut bank and fell into the shallow puddle she'd created by digging with her hoof. All three of us slurped, and I dug down farther to make a deeper hole. The water was muddy and stung my cut lips, but I didn't care. Drinking felt wonderful.

Once I got a couple of mouthfuls, I paused to

wonder if the water was safe to drink. It was full of sand; what else might be in it? But drinking right now was more important than worrying about getting sick. I took off the shirt around my head. "Here," I offered. "We can use this to filter it."

I spread the shirt out on the ground, and then wrapped up a wad of wet sand inside. When I hung the shirt over the tin can and squeezed hard, I was excited to see clear water trickle out.

"That's pretty smart," Martin said.

I felt a little glow in my heart. It had been a long time since Martin had said anything like that to me.

Once the can filled, Martin drank it. Martin held the shirt as I filtered a canful for myself, forearms aching from the effort. When I tipped the can into my mouth, the water was delicious going down my throat.

After we drank, the donkey trotted off. I was sad to see her go, especially since she helped save us. But we were too weak to try to catch or chase after her. Here in the wash, the cut bank was about as high as the basketball nets at school. It created shade. We scooped depressions down into the damp sand and sat with our backs to the bank. It was a stark relief from the burning sun, and I felt I'd never move again. Sighing, I took my goggles off and rubbed my eyes.

"I'm so thankful we had our donkey to help us find water," I said. "I don't know what would've happened without her."

Martin dropped his face in his palm and yelled, "She's a *burro!*"

I turned my head away to hide a grin.

We both heard a noise and looked up. I recognized the *thump-thump-thump* of a helicopter. They couldn't see us down here, hidden by the banks of the wash.

We scrambled out of our damp-sand seats and tried to scale back up into view. The more we rushed, the more our feet sank in the soft sand, slowing us down. The helicopter flew low, right over us, before we could climb to the top.

"Over here!" Martin jumped around, waving his arms.

I grabbed the wet shirt and waved it like a flag. But nobody saw us. The helicopter didn't come back.

CHAPTER ELEVEN

"NO!" we both yelled.

We watched the helicopter move farther away. Once it was almost out of sight, it began doing low circles. I threw the T-shirt to the ground. They'd never see the shirt anyway. It was earthy-tan, the same color as everything around me. Martin fell to his knees and hung his head.

"We should've grabbed the mirrors off our bikes," I said, realizing too late that Martin's book had called them lifesavers. "We could've used them as signaling mirrors. That's one of the most important things to have in an emergency."

"Now you say it? Really?" Martin jumped up and pointed at me. "Smarty-Pants, Think-You-Know-Everything-in-the-World, couldn't think to mention that when we were back at the bikes?"

"You were on that page for, like, five minutes. I'm not the only one who read about the signal mirrors!" I yelled back at him.

"Yes, you are! You are the only one who read it because I couldn't read it!"

"I'm sick of you being so mean . . . Wait . . . What?" I stammered, confused. "What do you mean you couldn't read it?"

Martin was silent for a moment. All the fight and anger seemed drained out of him. "I wish I was as smart as you," he said, so softly I almost missed it.

"You're smart," I said.

"No, Jen. I have to work hard for everything. Like reading. I can't understand the words if they're too long, or if they're all squished together small like in a grownup book." Martin kicked a rock and refused to meet my shocked gaze. "I didn't know what you were talking about earlier, when you said you'd read stuff in my book, because I didn't read it. I was just looking at the pictures."

"You were *what?*" That didn't make any sense. I'd grown up with Martin. I knew everything about him.

"That's why I like Club so much," he continued. "I understand how the coordinates and the GPS work. I like numbers. They're easy. It's just not fair how much I have to work at reading. *Everything* comes easily to you. You read something once, and you remember it." His voice grew louder as he went on.

"And then you joined Club too, the one thing *I'm* good at. You ruined it. That's why I stopped being your friend. That's why I'm always trying to beat you to the caches. I wanted to be better than you at *one thing*." He finally looked at me.

"But you couldn't let me, could you? You're always trying to be better."

We both stood motionless in the silence left behind by the helicopter.

"I thought . . . I didn't know . . ." I avoided his eyes while I tried to think about what to say. "I'm sorry. But really . . . you have trouble reading? Are you *sure?*" I could hardly believe him.

He threw me a look that made my face burn even without the sun, and I looked away. "We should . . . um . . . stay here in case the helicopter comes back. But we need shade. I'll go find wood to build some kind of shelter."

I watched Martin turn and stomp toward the crop of willows and shrubs.

How could I have missed that he had trouble reading? I thought back to all the projects we'd shared and worked on together. He hid it well. He did things like pretend to read books when other people were around.

The desert sun scorched down on my bare head. I bent to retrieve Martin's T-shirt and wrapped it over me again. It was cool and gritty with mud. I peered down at the shade near the water, longing to go back. But we couldn't stay down there again. No one would see us. What we needed to do was make an SOS sign with rocks.

I scanned the open area at the top of the wash. Yes, right here. And then we could sit and wait to be rescued. We had water now. Martin was right; we needed shade.

"Hey, Martin, remember when we went to the Tucson Desert Museum?" I yelled.

"So? I think I've seen enough of the desert."

"Could we make one of those shelters they had for shade, do you think?"

Martin was silent a minute. "No. They anchored their poles into the dirt to support the roof. The ground out here's too hard to dig."

I pondered the problem. How were we going to get out of the sun but still stay out in the open for searchers to find us? I thought about a picture I'd seen, showing huts made out in the open like this . . . yeah. We could make a tepee. All the poles supported each other. We wouldn't need to dig.

Martin came out of the shrubs, dragging two wood stalks taller than him. I went to help. "Perfect. If we can find one more, we can make a tepee."

Martin dropped the stalks and peered around.

"We can use the stalk from that yucca over there." I picked my way past a toothy bush and reached the plant with long green fronds. A tall stalk the color of oats grew upright from the center. I grabbed the stalk and snapped it off. Then I dragged the stalk back, noticing how tired and lightheaded I still felt. Since we'd gotten so dehydrated, we needed to stop working and drink more. But the helicopter was going to return, and soon we'd have all the cold, refreshing water we needed.

I dropped the stalk next to the others. "When

the searchers come back, we should lie flat on the ground; we'll be easier to see than if we're standing. I read about it . . . in a book once . . ." I trailed off.

Martin narrowed his eyes at me. Then he bent and pulled the lace out of his right shoe. We tied the ends of the poles together and set them upright against each other. We braced the ends on the ground with rocks so the frame was sturdy.

"Now what?" Martin asked, studying the poles.

I thought about the photos I'd seen. "If we tie willow branches sideways along the middle, we can weave fronds and willow into the frame to fill it in and block out the sun."

Our project gave us the chance to avoid talking or looking at each other. Martin used his other shoelace to tie the horizontal branches, but we were running out of string.

I pulled my earbuds out of my pocket. "I

wonder if I can use the cord to tie this branch with," I said.

Martin's eyes went big when he saw what was in my hand.

"Why didn't you say you had those?" He grabbed them from me, searching the ground wildly.

"What?" I asked. "What are you doing?"

"All this time," he muttered to himself. He found a rock and smashed one of the earpieces.

"Hey! I was only going to use the cord, not break them!"

The earbud split in half, and its insides spilled out. Martin reached in and pulled out a tiny round piece with a black ring around it. He held it up. "I've been trying to figure out what we could use for a magnet, when all this time you had one in your pocket."

I stamped my foot. "Martin, what are you talking about?"

He blinked at me and pulled the Snake Byte

coordinate sheet out of his pocket. He ripped the staple off the paper and held it up next to the earbud. "We're going to make a compass and get out of here."

CHAPTER TWELVE

I stumbled after Martin, back down to the dried riverbed, our partially finished shelter forgotten. "How? How can you make a compass?"

He stopped to pick up a dried leaf from the ground before kneeling beside our tiny pool of water. "Mom and I made one at home once. But we used a paper clip, a fridge magnet, and a cork. All this time, I was trying to figure out where to find a magnet out here." He chuckled as he straightened the ends of the staple.

"I didn't even know there was a magnet in my earbuds," I said.

I watched as he held the metal staple and rubbed it against the magnet as if he were lighting a match. "You need to do about fifty strokes," he explained, counting quietly to himself. Finally he held up the staple. "Now it's magnetized."

He placed the staple on the leaf in the center of the still pool. We both gasped as the staple and leaf began to slowly spin on top of the water.

"It's working!" I said.

"It's being pulled by the earth's magnetic field," Martin said, his eyes dancing with hope.

"I wasn't sure if it would work again, but look!" He pointed at it.

The staple stopped and held its position.

Martin indicated where the staple pointed. "That's the north-south line. The sun rose somewhere over there this morning." He waved with his left arm. "That's east. That means behind us is magnetic north. Now we just need to figure out true north. We're about eight degrees east declination here. So I'd say that's true north." He waved slightly off from where the staple pointed.

I stood. "What? Eight degrees east? That's not right. North is north. I've never heard of 'declination.'"

Martin dropped his arm and stared at me. "What are you talking about? How can you be a geocacher and not know the difference between magnetic north and true north?"

I shaded my eyes and searched the horizon where he pointed. "The GPS tells me where to look," I said. It sounded lame.

"Seriously? Look, just trust me. From the map we drew of the road location, we know that we're supposed to be heading southeast. So when we factor in the declination, that's where we need to go." He pointed.

I checked the staple again. "The compass says that southeast is this way."

"Jen, a compass points to magnetic north. Declination is the difference between magnetic north and true north. For this area, the declination is eight degrees east. So we just subtract eight degrees from magnetic north and that's how to get true north."

This was a big decision. I didn't want to get something this important wrong. We had to know exactly which direction to go; otherwise, we might walk parallel to a road for miles and not even know it. We could die out here. Suddenly I was too afraid to go anywhere.

"I'm not sure. And the helicopter is coming back," I insisted. "We can't leave."

Martin sighed and took off his hat, rubbing his hands through his short dark hair. He peered at the horizon as if he could make a road appear now that we knew which direction to travel. Kneeling, he plucked the staple from the leaf and put it back in his pocket.

"Maybe you're right. We've got water here. Let's stay for the rest of the day in case they come back. But if they don't come, we'll leave in the morning."

While we waited for rescue, we made a giant SOS sign out of rocks on the ground. I kept scanning the sky and listening for helicopters. All I saw was a dust devil off in the distance. It was nothing like the storm that had driven us here. I watched as a spiral of dust rose up a couple hundred feet into the air. It spun for a moment until it fizzled out and scattered.

I tied my goggles back on when my eyes started to ache again. Martin said his hat was good enough, but I suspected it was because he was worried about me.

To finish the shelter, we used the Clovis point to slice at the flexible willow branches. "We can use these to weave between the horizontal branches and the poles of the tepee," I said. "I'll fill in the bottom part and leave a space for the door. You fill in the top section."

By the time we weaved the last of the branches into the frame of our tepee shelter, daylight was already fading. The desert glowed in the

soft light. My stomach pinched and felt caved in suddenly. In the heat of the day, I wasn't hungry. But now in the cooler air, and after we'd had something to drink, I noticed my hunger. It had been almost two days since we'd eaten.

Two days. We'd been lost a long time. Were our families all in Las Cruces, along with the search and rescue people? I had wanted to believe they'd spot us easily. Why hadn't they found us by now? But I knew. We'd made the mistake of moving around after we realized we were lost. What if we were so far gone now that no one would ever find us? My throat tightened. I could not die out here. I was going to get back home to my family. I was going to survive. We both were.

CHAPTER THIRTEEN

Martin and I collected grasses for the floor of the shelter to keep us out of the dirt. It was hardly big enough inside for both of us to squeeze in.

"We're not going to be cold like last night," Martin said, lying down and taking up the whole floor. "Home sweet home."

"We survived another day." That sounded heavy once I'd spoken it. *Survived*. It was a scary word out here, not like at home, scrolling through TV shows like *Do or Die* or another season of *Survivor*. This was real. Were we going to die out here? How were we going to survive another day? Martin sat up, and I crawled in next to him. We both looked out at the darkening sky in silence.

"They've already searched this area. You know they're probably not coming back here, right?" Martin said. He was interrupted by the sound of coyotes.

"Again?" I cried, and crawled out toward the spot I had prepared for a fire.

Using the Clovis point and steel to make a fire was easier now that I'd figured out the technique. This time we already had a rock wall built on three sides to protect our tinder from the wind. Martin ripped more paper off the Snake Byte coordinate list and balled it up for the sparks to land on. After a few strikes, a thick spark leaped off and landed on the paper. I bent closer, breathing on it carefully until it burst into flame. "Fire out of stone and steel," I murmured proudly.

A branch cracked, the same sound as last night. I whipped my head around and thought

I saw a gray donkey butt disappear into the willows.

"Must've been the burro last night too," Martin said. "She's either strangely attracted to fire, or she's following us."

"I don't mind her following. I think she's watching out for us," I said, ducking back into the shelter.

The night noises began with clicking and hooting. I heard a tiny *crunch-crunch-crunch* somewhere beside us. The coyotes howled nearby, but this time it wasn't so scary. Not with our shelter and fire. In fact, their songs seemed completely right, out here in this big lonely place. I'd thought it looked empty without the big cacti from the Sonoran Desert back home, but now I saw how this desert was filled with its own beauty.

I thought again about heading back out across all that space tomorrow. Martin was better at numbers than me. I could trust him to know about declination.

"We should follow your compass," I told Martin. "You're usually right about stuff like that. Like, how did you know how the windmill worked? I wouldn't have known to turn it on. And I certainly didn't know about making a compass out of a magnet. I have a good memory, but you've been figuring things out for so long that you *know* things. That's better than memorizing." I nudged his arm shyly. "If we work together, we can figure out anything."

Martin finally smiled at me the way he used to when we were friends. I didn't know how much I missed that smile until I saw it. I smiled back as the tension left the space around us. I could feel our old friendship coming back to life.

Martin poked me in the arm. *"Goodness, gracious."*

"Great balls of fire!" I let out a chuckle and poked him back.

My smile turned grim as I looked out at the endless stars. I missed my family. I missed my home. I missed being able to turn on a tap whenever I was thirsty or dive into the pool when I was hot. I missed being safe.

Would we ever get back?

By the time a filtered pink light began in the sky, we were ready to go. The helicopter had not returned. We were going to find our own way back.

My head felt better. I made sure we had the can full of water, my goggles, my T-shirt on my head, and our compass. We headed out once again into the desert. But this time, by lining up our compass, minus declination, we pointed to one of the far ridges. It dipped in the middle like a chair. We planned to keep it right in front of us as we walked.

We marched on, determined. The desert looked different today. Instead of a big dead thing, I saw it was filled with life.

We walked for a long time, not talking. We

conserved our energy, kept our mouths closed, tried not to sweat, took sips of water. Martin looked behind me suddenly and froze. I glanced back and felt adrenaline charge through me.

CHAPTER FOURTEEN

"Oh, no!" I yelled.

Another storm was taking shape. The clear blue of the sky above us highlighted the dark, ominous clouds stalking behind us. A monstrous wall of dust and debris ripped across the desert with dizzying speed. It was nearly here.

"Memorize where the landmark is," Martin screamed just as the dust hit. Martin covered his head with his arms.

I tucked my chin down and stared at the southeast point. The storm monster roared toward us like a train. Once again, sand and dust swept over us, and we were engulfed.

I closed my eyes. Felt the sting and the lash of grit against my bare arms. The wind howled in my ears as if it knew we were trying to leave and it didn't want us to escape. Ten thousand tiny sharp needles hit my face and neck. The taste of grit filled my mouth. I held my breath.

But when I opened my eyes a little, I was surprised I could still see. My sand goggles were protecting my eyes from most of the blowing sand.

I grabbed Martin's hand and dragged him forward. I knew which way to go. I led him as he stumbled, clutching onto my hand and arm. He was yelling, but I couldn't hear over the storm.

I struggled to stay on the path while the howling wind blew sand into my ears. I stopped to pull the T-shirt down to protect them. It was only for a second that I'd looked down, but when I tried to find my landmark again, I realized it was gone.

I cranked my head around, desperate. How had I lost it that quick? Nothing but dust! We were in the middle of the chaotic fury. The way the bits of grass and twigs screamed past my view made me dizzy. Which direction should I go?

That's when I saw it. A shadowy form just ahead. What was *that?*

A four-legged shadow appeared in front of me. Was that a long face with tall ears? Was that our donkey? I tried to touch her, but the shadow moved just out of reach.

I took one step forward. Then another. Martin squeezed my hand, and I pulled him with me. Dust found its way up my nose, down my throat. I clamped my lips together tightly, fighting back. We were going to get through this.

I shuffled toward the donkey, stumbling when the ground sloped under me. I moved down the slope carefully, keeping Martin's hand in my grip. When I peered up again, there were many shapes around us. What was this?

The dust storm was weakening. As I looked around, I could distinguish the shapes clearer. Was that a truck? I glanced at my feet.

Black asphalt, yellow stripes. We were standing on a highway. Cars were parked all along the side of the road. We had emerged from the desert right next to an old pickup truck.

"Martin," I whispered.

Martin raised his head and looked around just as the driver of the truck saw us.

The driver's eyes widened and his mouth hung open. *"¡Fantasmas del desierto!"* he murmured.

I took off my sand goggles and caught my reflection in the window of the truck. T-shirt wrapped around my head. A coating of dust all over me, except for the light band around my eyes where the goggles had been. An empty tin can clutched in one hand, and my best friend clutched in the other. Both of us dirty and sunburned and peeling.

I turned to the man who thought we were desert ghosts. "Can we use your cell phone?" I asked.

CHAPTER FIFTEEN

Tucson. Two months later.

"Wow." The reporter's voice seemed to break the spell of my story. He reached for his phone to stop recording. He shook his head as if to come out of the Chihuahuan Desert.

"That's my granddaughter." Ye Ye grinned as he winked at me. "She wows everyone she meets. Even the folks from the New Mexico Office of Archaeological Studies."

"Yes," the reporter said. "What happened to the Clovis point? May I see it?"

I shook my head. "The archaeologists have it. You're not supposed to remove artifacts, but it did save our lives."

I reached down and plucked Jack off the floor as he crawled over my feet. Burying my nose in his hair, I took a moment to think about everything I'd learned in the desert. How important my family and friends were to me, and how they kept me going.

"We're okay with the archaeologists, but we're in trouble with Mr. Lee—and majorly with our parents. We got in trouble bigtime for leaving the van. And then when we got lost, all those people had to go out searching for us. Mr. Lee talked with our dads. Since my dad is a judge, he knows all kinds of ways we can serve our sentence for the community. We're still working volunteer hours picking trash out of the desert with the Arizona Wilderness Stewards."

"You both are? Wasn't it Martin's fault that you guys left, though?"

"Well, we both broke the rules." And friends stick together.

The desert is a little like friendship. It can be dangerous—everything has spines or teeth to hurt you and bite—but it is vibrant and makes you feel alive. It was worth the trouble.

"Your Ma Ma is right," said the reporter. "You are smart and strong! And what about Martin? Has he realized how smart he is, too?"

"Oh, boy, has he ever," I said. "He got a new tutor over the summer who has helped with reading. We go back to school next week, and he's thinking he's going to be the smartest boy in seventh grade."

The reporter smiled and reached for a cream puff.

"Smartest *boy*," I repeated.

He chewed thoughtfully. "One more question about that second dust storm. Do you think the shape you saw was the donkey who guided you to the highway?"

"Well, I like to think she was our desert

guardian. But I think what guided us was how Martin and I worked together as a team and figured out where to go."

The reporter nodded and scribbled something down in his notebook.

"And she's actually a burro," I added. "But don't tell Martin I said that."

AUTHOR'S NOTE

One of the reasons I began researching for a desert story was hearing about two separate recent tragedies. Both involved tourists who perished under the hot sun. Tourists who were not used to a desert climate. The stories of how they died were even sadder when I learned of the circumstances—succumbing to dehydration while carrying water. Or trying to walk for help after a car became stuck on a back road. These stories deeply affected me because it seemed as if they could happen to anyone. A hike on a hot day doesn't sound so dangerous where I'm from.

I wanted to include a desert book in the Survivor Diaries series because I wanted to learn more about it. And I wanted to share desert safety tips with others who might not be familiar with the dangers.

I traveled to the area where this story takes place, interviewed members of the New Mexico Search and Rescue Council, hiked through arroyos, camped in the desert, and was mesmerized by the sounds, the smells, and the beauty of the landscape.

It was easy to find information about the well-known Sonoran Desert, but the Chihuahuan Desert intrigued me because not only was it challenging to find information on, but it's also one of the most diverse deserts in North America! It boasts more than 130 different kinds of mammals, 500 bird species, 3,000 plant species, and even 110 freshwater fish.

It's hard to imagine so much life in such an unforgiving landscape, but, as the saying goes, life finds a way. And I wanted to explore how the story's characters could find a way to live, like the animals who call the desert home. As I've learned while researching for this series, some people's survival seems to be due to a strong will to live. That remains a fascinating theme to explore. It begs the question, if this happened to me, what would *I* do? What would *you* do? Would you panic and give up, or would you stay focused and do what it took to fight and survive?

While this story was inspired by true events, some details are fictional, including the names of the characters and some of the places. And while you can find much information about wild burros in some parts of New Mexico, the presence of wild burros in the particular location where this story is set is imagined as well.

SO, WHAT SHOULD YOU DO IF YOU FIND YOURSELF IN A SIMILAR SITUATION?

SURVIVAL TIPS FROM THE NEW MEXICO SEARCH AND RESCUE COUNCIL

PLANNING A WILDERNESS TRIP

Prior to any trip, take the time to WRITE DOWN a comprehensive PLAN. Leave this plan with a reliable person who could notify the authorities on a timely basis in case of a suspected emergency. *In New Mexico, those authorities would be the New Mexico State Police.*

- Destination
- Departure time and date
- Expected return time and date
- Type of activities planned

- Needed supplies
- Needed clothing and footgear
- In-case-of-emergency considerations
- Personal description
- Vehicle description, plate number, and planned parking location
- Any medical or physical disorders; medications
- Cell phone numbers of you and anyone else with you

WHAT DO YOU DO WHEN HOPELESSLY LOST?

When you are hopelessly lost, do the following, UNLESS there are sound reasons to do otherwise:

1. **DO NOT PANIC!** Sit down, take several deep breaths, eat some food, drink some water, and take it easy until you calm down. Remember, people lost in the wilderness are typically found within 72 hours. If you have to move, mark your direction of travel in an

obvious fashion. It will make it easier for search and rescue teams to track you.

2. Stay in the location where you are rather than travel farther into the unknown. It is a lot easier for search and rescue teams to find a stationary subject than a moving one.

3. Send off emergency signals: THREE shots, and/or whistle blows. Pause, then repeat.

4. Make a fire IF conditions permit.

5. Stay as warm and dry as possible.

6. Make and consume warm/hot liquids as circumstances allow. Even hot water is good.

7. If necessary, make a very simple shelter. Protection from high winds and cold rain are the main concerns. In New Mexico, people can get hypothermia even in the hot sum-

mer. If there is sufficient snow cover on the ground, a simple hole scooped out and lined with vegetation, such as pine branches, will provide more warmth than exposed terrain. In cold climates, snow is an excellent insulator. Consider using the base of a large tree or overhanging rock.

8. Try your cell phone. You might successfully make a 911 call or send a text message even if you are not in your phone company's service area. All cell phone providers are required to let a 911 call through on their system. Try calling from a high area if it is safe to do so. And even if your phone has no reception, it can still be useful. If you hear a helicopter at night, it is probably out searching for you. The light from your screen could be used to attract its attention. Please conserve your battery.

9. And one more time — **DO NOT PANIC!**

TEN BARE ESSENTIALS OF
WILDERNESS TRAVEL

- Water
- Emergency food
- Topographic map, compass, GPS
- Sun protection: hat, sunglasses, sunscreen, emergency blanket
- Extra clothes: wool hat, gloves, socks, rain gear
- Signaling devices: whistle, signal mirror, and cell phone
- Flashlight with fresh batteries
- Knife, fire starter
- Matches, candle
- First-aid kit; include needles, thread, and safety pin

Survival tips courtesy of the New Mexico Search and Rescue Council

ACKNOWLEDGMENTS

In my research for this story, I relied upon many different sources of information. I'm grateful to the following people, who helped answer questions and steer me in the right direction. Any errors in this story are my own.

Mary K. Walker, search dog handler, New Mexico Search and Rescue Council Board, Chair. Vic Villalobos and Ned Tutor with the Mesilla Valley Search and Rescue team, Las Cruces. Staff at the Arizona-Sonora Desert Museum in Tucson, Arizona. Jake Dominy for the friendly guiding service. Bruce Tomlinson for GPS coordinate expertise. And thank you —as always—to my critique partners, Amy Fellner Dominy, Marcia Wells, Caroline Starr Rose, and Sylvia Musgrove.

ABOUT THE AUTHOR

Terry Lynn Johnson lives in Northern Ontario, Canada. She was previously the owner and operator of a dogsledding business with eighteen huskies. She guided overnight trips and taught winter survival. During the school year, she taught dogsledding at an outdoor school near Thunder Bay, Ontario.

She currently works as a conservation officer with the Ontario Ministry of Natural Resources and Forestry, a job she's had for seventeen years, patrolling the outdoors across Ontario. Before becoming a conservation officer, she worked for twelve years as a canoe ranger warden in Quetico Provincial Park, a large wilderness park in Northwestern Ontario.

In her free time, Terry enjoys kayaking, camping, fishing, hiking, snowshoeing, skiing, and traveling to new places.

Stay calm. Stay smart. Survive.

Watch out for more books in the
SURVIVOR DIARIES series at survivordiaries.com!

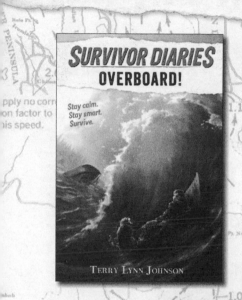

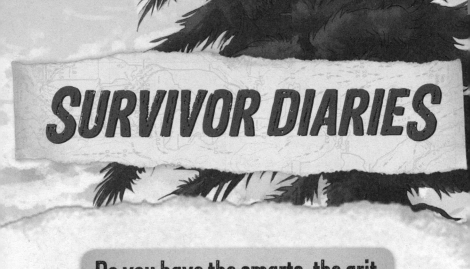

SURVIVOR DIARIES

Do you have the smarts, the grit, and the courage to survive?

— or —

Are you better off staying home?

YOU'VE READ THE BOOK, NOW PLAY THE GAME.
WILL YOU SURVIVE?

survivordiaries.com

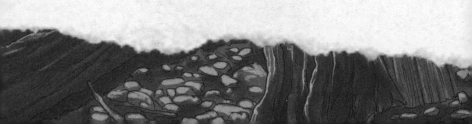